beach vibes

MADISON MCSWEENEY

ANUCI PRESS

First paperback edition January 2024
By Anuci Press www.anuci-press.com

Cover design by Adrian Medina
Fabledbeastdesign.wordpress.com

ISBN 979-8-9896198-0-1 (paperback)

www.madisonmcsweeney.com

MY FIRST KISS was from a lifeguard, and it was followed by chest compressions.

The water is teal, bright as a neon sign, gently oscillating, and when I go under I see schools of slim, glinting fish flitting by almost too fast for the eye to catch. Emboldened by the cheap plastic goggles shielding my eyes, I venture farther from the shore, to where the water is deeper and colder. It's my first time swimming in the ocean, and "watch out for the undertow" is never a phrase I've had to consider the practical implications of.

I flail wildly as the riptide grabs me, and my goggles fly off. I shut my eyes just before the water can rush in, and open them again to blackness. A moment of blind terror, and then a light winks on in the distance. *The* light, I think, with a muted panic as it comes closer. Following – no, attached to it – is a grey fish shaped like a skull.

The creature's eyes defy the darkness, shimmering with a kaleidoscope of crystalline purples and blues – colours that shouldn't exist at these depths. Its spiked tail is an icy fringe, and its gaping jaw reveals rows of long, dagger-like teeth. *Angler fish*, I think, remembering the term from the *Planet Earth* documentaries they show in science class. The kind that lives at the darkest depths of the ocean, where the only light is what comes from the fish itself. The sense of recognition reassures me before curdling into a more terrifying question: *just how deep have I sunk?*

I forget that I can't breathe and dive even deeper.

The water here is so dark that I can't see my own arms as they pull me forward, downward. Every so often, another monster fish floats by; without the context of my surroundings, it's impossible to tell how close they are, or how large, though several look like they could outweigh me. Some are round and balloon-shaped, hideous bulging faces with pitifully small tail fins added as an afterthought. Others are long and skinny, their snakelike bodies rippling with rainbows of luminescence. Still others come in even stranger shapes, designs I've never seen in nature, formed without regard to aerodynamics or aesthetics. The glowing orbs they carry illuminate rocky protrusions and subterranean caverns that line the ocean floor; sometimes they light each other's way, but mostly, they travel alone.

As I get closer to the bottom of the crater, the number of visible lights increases. This must be where they congregate, perhaps to spawn (or to sleep, if such things sleep at all) among the stalagmites. I find myself drawn towards the caves – not by any force of the water, for the undertow has long since surrendered me, but by their pull on my mind. My rational mind tells me that if I'm not dead already, this is the place that will kill me; the subterranean hole where I will be trapped and starved of air, or from whence a monster will shoot out and ensnare me. But the buried part of my brain promises wonders.

I'm hovering at the mouth of a cave, gripping one of its

jagged teeth with a hand so numb that I barely feel anything as the rock breaks the skin. I've long since stopped wondering why I'm still conscious. Nor does it strike me as strange that I'm hearing human voices – or else something not quite human, an ethereal choir singing to me, calling me deeper. But just as I kick my legs to cross the threshold, a clammy hand grabs my foot and pulls me out.

* * *

"Skylar, you okay?"

Shanelle is shaking me awake, glossy magazine slipping off her lap.

"Yeah," I say, blinking. My vision is still blurred from sleep, my friends out of focus. The steady hum of my mind's ocean has been replaced by the mechanical whirring of the plane, which reminds me of being in a walk-in freezer.

Passengers strapped in two-by-two like an assembly line on either side of me. Lots of sleeping old people. To my left, by the aisle, is Shanelle, her hand still on my arm like she forgot to remove it after jolting me out of the dream world. In front of us, heads twisted to peer through the gaps between the seats, Jamie and Brooke. Jamie's dark hair is scrunchied back and Brooke has sunglasses already perched on her head, even though she hasn't needed them at all for this leg of the trip. It was still dark when we left for the airport.

"You look white," Brooke says.

"Yeah, girl, you don't look great at all," Shanelle adds.

"I told her to take a sleeping pill," Jamie reminds us.

"She *was* sleeping."

"I always used to be a bad flyer," says someone I don't know, a middle-aged woman in a visor seated in the adja-

3

cent row. "I take an anti-anxiety pill now before I get on the plane."

"I just had a weird dream," I assure them, as if that makes any sense to anyone other than me. I redirect the conversation to my friends, angling myself away from the interrupting woman. "Was I talking to myself?"

"A bit, yeah," Shanelle replies.

Jamie nods vigorously. "You were making some weird noises."

"Ugh." At least I wasn't saying actual words.

I feel more embarrassed than I rationally should, in this situation. I'm sort of stung by the implication that I'm a bad flier. It's not flying that's the problem.

Five rows ahead, a uniformed stewardess is pushing a metal cart that barely fits in the aisle. "Excuse me," Jamie chimes, in that effervescent customer service voice. "Could my friend get a ginger ale? Her stomach's a little upset."

"Be with you in a minute," she calls back, in the middle of pouring tea for the passenger she's actually serving. As an afterthought, she adds: "There's a sick bag in the seat pocket."

Brooke rolls her eyes and faces forward again, reclining her seat – which is directly in front of mine and only makes me more claustrophobic. "Only Skylar could get seasick 35,000 feet above sea level."

"Screw off, Brooke."

* * *

If my bright yellow swim goggles hadn't floated to the surface, they never would have found me in time. That was ten years ago, and I've never forgiven the water. The last time I tried to let my guard down, I ended up hyperventilating on my back in the lobby of a wave pool. So how my girlfriends dragged me to the edge of the ocean for spring break, I'll never understand.

There were a thousand reasons, of course. Shanelle being accepted into the psychology program – *we have to celebrate.* Jamie tending her wounds from that break-up – *this'll be good for her.* Brooke wants to lie in the sun and meet boys – *and what fun is that without her girls? You don't have to go anywhere near the water,* they said, even as they were booking beachfront accommodations.

Standing on a Juliet balcony on the fourteenth floor of a four-star hotel, I am as close to the water as I'm ever comfortable being. The sky is black as ink, but the beach below is crowded with tourists, trolling the shoreline with flashlights as they search for the elusive perfect shell. From where I stand, they look like the bioluminescent fish that live along the ocean floor, glowing bulbs dangling from cartilaginous stalks. The tide roars towards the shore at their feet, stifled waves gnashing their teeth.

Of course, the perfect shell no longer exists – at least, not for just anybody. The ornate striped cockles and colourful coquina clams, the conchs you can put your ear to and hear the sea in, were all collected long ago, brought home by decades of tourists or harvested by souvenir shops. The ones that remain are identical, tiny, and as pure white as pearls. *One day,* I muse, *the Hilton will monetize the collection of shells along the beach, and that will be the day the sea rises up to reclaim the shore.*

I shake my head, expelling the idea like water in my ears, and retreat from the window. My phone has been charging on the bedside table for the past hour and is barely at thirty percent. The heat kills the battery; it was almost down to zero when I plugged it in. No messages from Blake – I guess he's done with talking. Fair enough; it's nearly ten o'clock, and he works an early shift. I post some photos and scroll through Instagram for a few minutes, before remembering that I have my own picture-perfect panorama available to me for a limited time. Back to the window.

How perfectly cloudless the sky is. You never get views like where I'm from – even on the sunniest days, the kind of blissful summer afternoon that prompts people to cry out, "Not a cloud in the sky!", there's always a wispy one drifting at the margins. Here, by contrast, it's easy to imagine the void as a solid black curtain shielding us from a realm of blinding light, the stars just a million tiny puncture wounds.

There aren't many of those on display tonight – a respectable number, but not nearly as many as you'd see in a truly isolated area. Light pollution. I'm glad to be fourteen floors up, spared from the glare of whatever spotlights the hotel staff leave on to prevent guests from killing themselves on their way to the beach.

As if in mockery, a new source of light tugs at the corner of my eye. I look up to see a radiant orb dangling above my head. Fear ricochets through my body – the primal fear that kicks in an instant before the more developed part of the brain can supply rational reasons to be afraid. *A plane, out of control, hurtling towards my hotel.* But the object is farther away than a plane should be, and it doesn't appear to be moving. *The moon then, at an odd angle.* But neither the shape nor size is right; it's ovular like a lightbulb and, visually, about the size of my fist. Much bigger than anything else in the sky.

"Who are you?" I say aloud, not expecting a reply.

I realize that my initial impression – of the object as

stationary – was also wrong. The light is bobbing, like a buoy on a still lake. I keep my eyes on the thing, but it doesn't come any closer, and soon enough a black mist drifts over to cloak it.

I guess there are clouds here after all.

* * *

The beach is beautiful in an otherworldly sort of way. The trees are exotic, almost alien, with thick, spiky trunks and pineapple-shaped crowns; not lithe or slender like the palms I've seen in cartoons, but squat and swollen like ticks gorged on blood. The blinding white sand stretches to the horizon on all sides, dotted with identical white umbrellas rented from the hotel for absurdly inflated prices.

My friends and I eschew the umbrellas and make do squinting under cheap dollar store sunglasses. I prop myself up semi-comfortably on a pink and blue beach towel, well back from the beach, trying in vain to find a comfortable position to read in. I look over my shoulder at the sandy incline leading back up to the hotel deck. Maybe if I relocate there, I can have some semblance of back support.

"You're not going in the water?" Shanelle, shielding her eyes with her hand.

"Nah," I say, settling back on the towel. "I'm still not feeling a hundred percent."

She cocks her head sympathetically. "Wait, are you actually sick?"

"Just a little bit of heat stroke."

A knowing smirk crosses her face. "So, that's why you didn't come out last night. We all thought you were just pining."

I smile. "Well, a little of that too."

Savvy enough not to pry further, she changes the subject. "What are you reading?"

I twist my arm to show her the book cover. "It's a memoir," I say. "About a poet whose father was a Catholic priest."

She raises her eyebrows. "You do you, girl," she replies, before jogging back to the water.

The heat stroke thing is a bit of a lie. It was true last night, when I opted out of a bar-hopping marathon in favour of tap water and air conditioning, but today I'm completely recovered. But the ocean seems nastier today. In the distance, well-muscled spring breakers attempt to surf only to wipe out and fall face-first into the bubbling foam. I wince as I watch my friends throw themselves into the pulsing waves, surrendering to them, riding to the crests, freeing themselves an instant before the undertow can smother them. I self-consciously return to my book, if only for something else to look at.

I wish we hadn't come here. I can't breathe in this heat. I find myself re-reading the same lines two, three times over, losing focus as I fixate on taking deep lungfuls of air that only make me hungrier for it. *Is this what a panic attack feels like?* Mid-page turn, I scramble to avoid an errant frisbee, which comes hurtling towards me with lethal force. The thrower smiles at me as he retrieves it; I return the look to be polite, but not so enthusiastically that he might think I'm flirting. In other circumstances I may have, but I'm currently at the flirting and sexting stage with the absent Blake, and I can only focus on one boy at a time.

That's the thing about love – it stunts the imagination. I used to be able to daydream all sorts of futures for myself, strange winding paths that I can follow to the horizon and over, but whenever I come close to making a decision, it's like I'm suddenly staring down a tunnel.

"Heads up!"

"Yo, man, you almost beamed her."

Maybe I should have turned on just a little charm, as the frisbee guys have lost all regard for me. After the third near miss, I gather my stuff. The sand further back from the water is dotted with cigarette butts and bottle caps, but I eventually find a semi-clear spot near the top of the incline. I'm rearranging my towel when a gust of wind sprays dirt in my eyes.

I raise a hand to my face just as the torrent begins, battering the seas and sending whirling tornados of sand and salt across the beach. Pages flutter, and I pull my book closer to my chest. In the distance, tourists shriek and scramble to save towels and umbrellas and shovels and pails from the gale, which rips my sunglasses off my head. I don't go after them. As the windstorm intensifies, I'm doused by an icy rain, which I soon realize is not water from the sky but the sea rising up. I start to panic for my friends, still submerged in that churning ocean, dragged beneath the waves and drowned, under the undertow, screaming and swallowing water, choking and sputtering, dragged into dark places filled with glowing freaks, lured even deeper by the sound of...

The wind stops.

I wait a moment for the sand to settle before opening my eyes. The other tourists have already collected their things and resumed their leisure, recovering so quickly that the whole storm may well have been a hallucination. The only hard evidence is the detritus scattered across the beach, and the more aggressive sloshing of the waves. Scanning the beach, I locate my friends by the neon of their suits – Shanelle in her hot pink two-piece, Brenda in blue, and Jamie in a neon-green bikini, her white skin like marble against the dark water. In contrast to the pale aqua of the rest of the visible ocean, the area where my friends float is grey, as if a massive shadow has been cast over the water. I look up. There is truly not a cloud in the sky.

Huh.

As the ocean calms, the image comes into sharper relief. There's something under the surface of the water, not more than a few metres below the dangling feet of my friends. *Sea monster* is the word that comes to mind, and I can't think of anything better.

They must see it, I think, even though that's clearly not the case. I wait for it to move, either flit away back to the depths or take a snap at the swimmers, but it lingers. I could almost write it off as an optical illusion, silt and sand and weeds from the sea floor whipped up by the storm, if it weren't for the gaping, wide set eyes – at least fifty feet between them – angled inward and trained separately on Jamie's feet and the starfish that is Brenda.

And as I hesitate, the image changes again. At first, I think it's the water rippling, but the surface is still; it's just one edge of the creature that seems to bristle with retractable spikes. *Teeth.*

Abandoning my book and towel, I burst into a headlong run down the hill, heedless of the hot sting of the rocks against my bare feet. Heads turn my way and I realize I'm screaming, my cries as soundless to me as they were that day under the water, but loud enough for everyone else to hear just fine: "Get out of the water!"

My friends see me. I see their heads pop up and swivel towards me, and suddenly they're no longer lounging. "Get out!" I yell again, even as the words hit the wall at the edge of the ocean. No matter. Shanelle is swimming to shore, propelling herself with the long, steady strokes of an experienced swimmer, with Jamie close behind. Brenda doesn't move, but watches alertly from a purple inflatable ring. I get to the shore just as Shanelle reaches it from the other direction. "What's wrong?" she demands, grabbing me by the shoulders as if to shake me.

I brush her off and point. "There's a—"

Shanelle follows my hand. Her brow furrows. "What are you seeing?"

I can't bring myself to articulate what I'm seeing, so I gesticulate again. "Under the surface!" I insist, as if that makes any more sense than saying *sea monster,* or *megashark* or *there's a man on the wing!*

She makes a show of narrowing her eyes to squint at the water, humouring me. "There's nothing there, Skylar."

"But I sa-" My voice tapers, and I gaze out over the sea again to find it clear and blue, as placid and cloudless as the sky above.

* * *

"I don't have heat stroke," I say, putting down the glass of water Shanelle insisted I drink.

"I googled the symptoms and disorientation can be one of them," Shanelle insists. I resist the urge to tell her that if what I saw wasn't real, "disorientation" would be an understatement. "Apparently it can be really dangerous if left untreated. I'm just saying, it might be a good idea to get checked out."

The mattress squeaks as I sit on the edge of the bed. The sheets – like the rest of the room - are so clean they almost smell like chlorine. "Do you really want to spend half a day that we're paying for sitting in a hospital waiting room?"

She doesn't reply, which is her answer. As an afterthought she throws out, "Well, we have travel insurance." But I know she won't push the issue any further. As far as Shanelle's concerned, she's discharged her liability.

"Brooke and Jamie seemed annoyed," I observe.

Shanelle starts fidgeting with a tube of sunscreen, struggling to squeeze the last few millilitres out of the flattened tube. I suspect she's trying to avoid meeting my eyes. "We're just worried about you."

I laugh. "Bullshit."

She throws up her hands. "Okay, it was a little embarrassing. I don't know if you saw back there, but everyone was looking at you."

Of course, I saw.

"What does that matter?" I ask. "It's not like we'll be running into these people again."

She shrugs. "I think Brooke and Jamie are trying to pick up guys. And that's hard to do if they're seen as being with the crazy girl."

"Nice." I take a swig of the water. It's lukewarm and, given the humidity here, like drinking sand. "They don't seriously think they're going to have some romantic summer fling, right? Does that ever happen outside of the movies?"

"You know them. They've been building this trip up for weeks. It needs to be their insta-perfect dream vacation or it's a failure."

"Then why'd they invite me?" I ask.

"Don't be like that."

"I'm not being like anything." I duck into the little bathroom and dump out the water glass, filling it up again after

I've run the cold tap. "I don't like the water, so I don't know why I was strong-armed into coming to a trip that's ninety-nine percent swimming."

"We can do fun things that aren't swimming," she protests.

I emerge, gulping the glass in one try. "There's a Pink Floyd laser light show tonight," I say pointedly.

Her face falls. "A what?"

"The planetarium will be playing the album *Dark Side of the Moon* in its entirety set to a psychedelic light show. And tomorrow they're doing the same thing with *The Wall*."

I see her bite her lip, searching for the words to let me down gently. "Okay, maybe not that," she finally says.

I buy an overpriced pair of sunglasses and spend the rest of the day exploring the strip, as much to get out from under the judgemental gazes of my friends as to check out the scenery. This has not been the female bonding trip I was hoping for: one day in, Jamie and Brooke are both embarrassed of me and Shanelle literally thinks I'm losing my mind.

"I think everyone hates me here," I text Blake at the height of my self-pity. He doesn't reply.

I pay twenty dollars to get into a kitschy pirate museum on the boardwalk, where we look at rotted wooden chests and hear grisly stories of spirits that claim drowned men for themselves, and the vengeance the sea takes against those who survive.

The museum is walled with old planks painted shit-brown; we're told they're from the former hull of a real-life pirate ship, but that's dubious. The guide is a superficially grizzled older man – introduced as simply "The Captain" - doing what must be a fake Nova Scotian accent. I'm not sure if that makes geographical sense, but the American tourists don't seem to question it.

"The year is 1767," the Captain tells us, chomping on an unlit pipe. "And pirates roam the seas." *The year is 2020*, I think, *and Skylar rolls her eyes*. I have to hold back a snort as he introduces a bloodthirsty seafarer literally named "Captain Morgan."

He's barely had a chance to start the tale before I feel my purse buzz. I unzip it and grope for my phone, bracing for a "Where are you???" text from one of the girls. Instead, it's Blake, responding to my last message, which looks more embarrassing now than it did when I sent it an hour ago. In any case, Blake's delayed response is cold comfort. "I'm sure they don't babe."

I smile and wince. Blake's bro-ey-ness is endearing enough in person but harder to stomach over text. I don't like being called "babe" or "girl" or anything like that. It feels generic and dehumanizing. And his grammar in writing – ugh.

I jump at the sound of the Captain's voice booming through the hall. "That's the sailor's destiny," he announces; "the sea always gets its man." I suspect he's speaking louder to get my attention.

"Thx," I text Blake back, quickly adding: "I humiliated myself today."

"oh yeah?"

I lag behind the rest of the tour group, the Captain glowering at me from behind a felt eyepatch, as I type an abbreviated version of the incident at the beach. It takes several rephrasings to make me sound reasonably sane. "It looked so real," I admit, remembering the eyes. "I can't believe there wasn't anything there."

"how do you know there wasn't?" Blake replies.

That throws me for a loop.

I'm now about six feet behind the back edge of the group. Ahead of us, the Captain is telling a story about an old-timey sailor who fell overboard during a storm. "The crew knew he was doomed, but the captain – a soft-hearted man, who didn't believe in the natural laws of the sea – this captain dove into the water and went after him..."

"bc it was there one instant, and then it wasn't," I write back, glad to have a distraction from these grim accounts of drowning and disaster. "Nothing that big can move that fast."

Blake doesn't reply, so the Captain has my undivided attention as he whispers, "The next morning – a calm morning, by all accounts, the ship capsized and sank, not stopping until she reached the bottom of the Atlantic. The entire crew drowned."

Three dots flash on my screen while Blake collects his thoughts. I wish he'd hurry up. I use the break to catch up with the tail end, stumbling over an upturned stretch of carpet like a jaywalking millennial.

His reply comes just as the Captain is asking, "Has anyone ever heard a Siren sing?" The message is longer than Blake's usual attention-deficit texts, and the spelling is so pristine I think someone's stolen his phone: "Philosophers and some physicists have a theory that there are infinite dimensions overlapping each other in the same physical space." The ellipsis re-appears. "And at some points they intersect."

"...the sea always gets its man, one way or another."

A shudder, as involuntary and inexplicable as a seizure,

rolls through me. I re-read the text and crinkle my nose, writing back, "Haha what?"

Blake replies with a wink emoji.

I don't know what to make of this. "Watching too much Discovery Channel?" I ask, adding an emoticon to soften the message.

After an eternity, he responds: "just tryna make you feel better babe."

I smile, trying to trick my body into shaking off the weirdness. Power poses: Brenda used to swear by them. *Fake it 'til you make it.* "I can't believe you're making fun of me in my time of need," I write back, because that would be a sensible explanation. When he doesn't reply for a moment, I add, "You're such a jerk," hoping to jolt him out of whatever weird mood he's in, bring us back into our usual rhythm.

I sigh in relief when he replies, "Why r u texting me thn? ;)"

"Maybe I like jerks. :)"

I slide my phone into my pocket and resolve to be scrupulously polite for the rest of the tour. The Captain's next story is a regional variation of the mermaid myth, and it's wholesome enough that even the description of a beautiful woman with clamshell breasts diving into the deepest depths of the ocean doesn't rattle me. I even find myself appreciating the evocative oil paintings of krakens menacing lighthouses and battered ships battling the thrashing waves.

Blake texts me again just as we're exiting the museum, emerging from the gloom back into the bright skies and exhaust fumes of the strip. "You need to get your mind off this," he advises sagely. "You should go to the beach and go for a swim." I frown. I've told Blake a thousand times that I don't like the water.

After a moment, his true intent becomes clear: "I want bikini pics."

I smile. "If you were here, I'd be skinny-dipping."

* * *

"Hey Shanelle – don't wait up for me. I'm still hitting the town."

* * *

"Are there any left for the Pink Floyd?"

"Fifteen dollars," replies the guy at the planetarium ticket booth, framed on either side by battered record sleeves taped to the window. He's about thirty, square-jawed, with thick brown hair slung over his shoulder in a greasy ponytail; he looks like he plays *Dungeons and Dragons*. He prints me a ticket as I slide my American bills beneath the transparent barrier. I find myself wondering why ticket sellers are always behind glass.

I tap the surface lightly, feeling it shudder. "Is that to protect you from us or us from you?"

"Huh?"

The joke made more sense in my head.

"Nothing," I reply, slinking away. "Thank you," I call back.

The auditorium is a sea of black band shirts and jeans. Aside from a pair of ten-year-old boys with their parents, I'm the youngest person in my row and, as far as I can see, the only solo woman – and based on the smell, one of the few audience members who hasn't pre-dosed on pot. I wonder if perhaps I've dropped the ball on that front, before reasoning that I don't even know how to buy weed back home, let alone in a foreign jurisdiction where I don't even know its legality. Gotta love the States.

The lights and music are hallucinogenic enough on their own, taking me out of my body and into some world that only makes sense if you're on LSD in post-war Britain. With my mood, the transportation amounts to a bad trip: I'm alone in a crowd again, hollow inside, feeling like no one has ever understood me, except maybe the guy who wrote "Brain Damage/Eclipse." As conquering tears well in my eyes, I'm glad this isn't *The Wall* show, because I think I'd bawl all through side three.

I can't be the only one crying, I think, as "Eclipse" nears its crescendo. It's a genuinely moving song, an affecting denouement. I wipe the moisture from my eyes, not wanting to compromise my view as the music fades out. One-by-one, the ruler-straight lasers blur together, vanishing to be replaced by a single spotlight, like all the colours in a rainbow travelling through a prism and emerging as pure white light. The house lights shut off at the same time as the music, and the last of the colour disappears.

The light is staring at me. At my sides, my hands clench into fists, and my eyes strain to make sense of the darkness beyond the light. I feel like I'm alone in a black abyss, suspended in the glare of an all-seeing eye. The room erupts in applause, and I remember that the cover of *Dark Side of the Moon* is a prism and that's the whole bit they're doing.

I start to clap. The colours return for a whirling, crazed finale, the last sequence of *Space Odyssey* on acid. Their choreography is synched not to music but to the sounds of planes, bombs, and gunfire, which I assume must be a poor-taste teaser for tomorrow's show. I'll definitely skip *The Wall*; I don't think I can handle it.

I walk out of the planetarium with my head down, avoiding eye contact with the ticket guy. When I get the nerve to scan the crowd, I *am* the only one crying.

* * *

Night takes me back to the beach, where I sit on the hill until the sun sets and the horizon disappears, and then head to the shore. The hotel behind me is a blurry behemoth, but ahead the sky is clear, the stars out in full force.

Tonight, the water's somehow tolerable. The ocean's at its worst when it's translucent: in the daytime, when you can just barely make out the outlines of horrible things beneath the surface – strangling seaweed, slimy fish, shells that cut like broken glass. In the dark it's not so bad, nearly indistinguishable from the sky. And if there has been a merger, the sky's come out ahead. The black water is speckled with its light.

In the middle of the panorama is the shining reflection of a disk that I mistake for the moon, before noticing the shape is off. I look up. Almost directly above my head, shining more brightly than the moon and hanging lower, is the unidentified object I saw last night. Whatever it is, it looks larger this time. Closer. Which is strange, considering I'm significantly closer to the ground than when I first saw it.

I glance over my shoulder to see the hotel lights starting to wink out. *Maybe I should go back,* I think, *before they all go dark.*

* * *

I dream again of drowning, but when I wake up, Blake is with me. Intertwined in stiff hotel sheets, he seems to touch every inch of my skin at once. His mouth clamps over mine, and suddenly there's no air in my lungs. My hand rises to meet his chest, my fingers sinking into the hair as I try to push him away, but my arm seems to go straight through him as his back arches and he retreats from me. I take a gulp of air, but the release is temporary; he's inside me again, his tongue filling my mouth, slithering into my throat and down my windpipe. I moan with pleasure, feeling his body merge with mine, our DNA intermingling like a million multicoloured grains of sand...

My eyes open, and it is cold.

I am lying on the beach, in a depression just deep enough to fit my body. Rectangular, about a foot or two deep: a shallow grave. A thin layer of sand has been smoothed over my torso like a blanket. The sky above is black and omnipresent, at once millions of miles away and pressing up against me. How did I end up here? I scan my brain, but all I remember in my post-dream state is turning around to head back to the hotel. Did I ever make it?

I lie in silent terror, knowing I could easily get up and leave but afraid to, as if there's something watching me, just out of sight, ready to pounce if I try to escape. There's no rational reason to believe that, except of course for everything I've experienced so far. Ever since I arrived at this beach, it's like the whole world's been playing a sick joke on me.

A joke. Of course.

My memory isn't yet cooperating, but my brain fills the gaps. I returned to the room, Brenda convinced me to take a few too many swigs from that souvenir flask she's so proud of, and when I passed out, they all carried me out here. Surely the three of them could lift me without much trouble, and since it was so late, they didn't have to worry about being seen. Was it late, though, when I went back to the hotel? So late that there were no other guests in the elevator or milling around the lobby? I think back to how many people were out that first night, wandering along the shore until nearly midnight.

Maybe I never went back to the room at all. Maybe they met me here, and we drank on the beach. That would make more sense, if I passed out here and they just left me. Still a dick move, but funny. Revenge for my freak-out yesterday. Fair enough. Possibly even a good thing. I'll return to the room, wake them all up as payback, and then we'll laugh about it and everything will be water under the bridge in the morning. My breathing feels lighter, even though I'm still partially buried. I sit up and brush the rocks off my arms, bending my knees to stand up. As I do so, the sand beneath my body collapses.

I fall a few feet and land with a thud on firmer ground. Three feet of sand boxes me in on all sides. I lurch into a seated position to pull myself out, but not before the walls collapse, covering me with a thick sludge. At the same time, the floor becomes wet and porous. My eyes sting, tears struggling to wash away the grains. When I raise a submerged hand to wipe them, the earth resists. *It's like a Chinese finger trap*, I think, before a more apt metaphor comes to mind: quicksand.

Or maybe it's not a metaphor.

I am drowning for real this time, but not in water. The more I struggle, the more unstable the ground underneath me becomes, and the deeper I sink. But whenever I stop struggling, more sand tumbles in from above, getting into my eyes, my nose, my throat, until I can no longer breathe, and soon everything is dark and I can't tell if it's because I have no oxygen or because I'm completely submerged.

With a burst of desperate strength, I punch through the canopy, freeing one arm. I grasp the first solid edge I can get a hand around, feeling the skin slice open and a wet warmth slide down my wrist. Then the sand rises and reclaims me.

I start to hear voices, muffled. At first, I think one of them is Blake's, his Southern Ontario bro twang filtering through layers of sediment, but it suddenly takes on a lilting tone, the Captain with his fake Cape Breton accent saying, "the sea always gets its man," and then it's shifting again, lightening into a girl's sweet tone, faint at first, and then suddenly very loud...

* * *

"Are you okay?"

I hear it through what feels like miles of sand, indistinct and unfamiliar. A female voice, but not any of my friends.

"...call someone?"

"She drunk?"

Three different voices, a Babel of conflicting accents. *Are they talking about me?*

"She's breathing," a man's voice chimes in, and kicks me.

My eyes fly open. Two men and one woman are looking down at me, like surgeons over an operating table. All well-built and strangely beautiful, chiselled abs and long, muscular arms and legs. They're leaning awkwardly against neon-coloured synthetic boards, already dressed for the beach even though the light behind them is dim. It's cold, still, and the sky's the pale grey-pink of dawn.

"What time is it?" I ask, able to think of nothing else.

The girl shrugs. "Six AM, about." She nervously pushes a thread of tightly curled blonde hair behind her ear. "Are you okay?"

"Yeah," I say, distractedly, trying to place her inflection. Swedish, maybe German. Her eyes are a bright, catlike green, staring at me intently.

"We thought you were a corpse, at first," blurts out one of the men. His accent is even stronger – he sounds like Arnold Schwarzenegger and looks like he could be a bodybuilder. The guy to his right elbows him in the ribs.

"Oww!"

"Idiot!"

Embarrassment starts to sink in. I've scared the shit out of these gorgeous foreign surfers. They probably assume I'm the drugged-out product of American decadence. Overcompensating, I force a smile and try to speak as lucidly as I can. "Thank you very much for waking me up," I say – and, lest they think I'm some sort of junkie, add: "I was stargazing last night and I must have fallen asleep."

"Happy to help," replies the elbower, as I climb shakily to my feet. I'm grateful that my clothes are mostly in place. The last thing my pride can handle right now is a wardrobe malfunction.

The bodybuilder brightens, his look of concern dissolving into a good-natured smile. "We wouldn't want you to get buried."

My heart stops. "What?"

A look of alarm crosses his face. "You know – one of those pranks. Someone falls asleep, they build on them the sandcastle" – he cups his hands across his chest – "with the breasts."

His face falls into an expression of horror as his friends both fix him with glares. I laugh drily to diffuse the tension, thank them again, and wipe the dirt off my legs. My hand leaves a red smear across my thigh.

* * *

"Where did you slink off to last night?" Shanelle asks, valiantly trying to hide a smirk.

"Just a walk on the beach," I reply, picking at the peeling edges of the Band-Aids criss-crossing my palm. The cut isn't that bad, but it bled like a mother when I presented it to the front desk, and no one bandage was large enough to contain the flow.

She raises both eyebrows, a provocative gesture. "Until 6 in the morning? I'm a light sleeper – don't think I didn't hear you come in."

"Mind your own business," I reply, trying my best to sound coy instead of confused and terrified. I could tell her that I was sleepwalking, but that would only freak everyone out. And they already think I'm nuts after my fit at the beach yesterday.

"Blake better watch out," Brooke chimes in, dragging a brush through her blonde hair.

"It's not like they're a thing yet," Jamie retorts, defending my conduct in an affair that has not occurred.

"Exactly!" I agree. "It's Spring Break, what do you expect me to do?" Let them think I went back to some tanned hunk's hotel room. I could use a few fun stories like that, anyway. I play it cool as the girls pepper me with questions ("Was it that guy with the frisbee? I saw him eying you") until they inevitably move onto other subjects.

Brooke is the first to get bored of the interrogation. "And it's not like Blake's been living like a monk," she blurts out, midway through wrapping an elastic around her ponytail. She may as well have slapped me. I see Shanelle's jaw clench, and Jamie's eyes are as wide open as her mouth, gaping like a fish.

"Excuse me?" I say. I mean to sound nonchalant about it, but the attempt to speak lightly causes my voice to crack.

Brooke's eyes dart across the room, landing on me and Jamie and then Shanelle, trying to gauge the extent of her fuck-up. She shrugs her shoulders. "Check out his Instagram story," she says.

Shanelle moves to restrain me, but I grab my phone off the nightstand, open the app and click on the thumbnail with his picture. The screen flashes with ten photos of Blake and some too-skinny bleached-blond stoner girl. Dancing with her at a nightclub, standing a little too close at a party, and, most incriminating of all, sitting out of frame, photographing her sipping a mimosa at the brunch place I once recommended to him. I go through the photo roll three times before dropping my phone on the bed, realizing why the girls are all so invested in me having a one-night stand. "So, you all knew," I say. It comes out more accusingly than I intended.

"You're not, like, a thing yet," Jamie repeats, all traces of *rah-rah-you-go-girl* leached from the words.

"No," I reply. "I guess not."

* * *

Halfway down the beach, a little boy is digging a hole, rejoicing as it spontaneously fills with water. I gaze pointedly in the other direction, a wave of nausea washing over me.

I think about my plane ticket, and how much this week in a hotel is costing me, even split four ways. When I agreed to come here, I deluded myself into thinking I'd face my fears and eventually hit the water. Now, sitting on dry land for the third day in a row, I'm calculating how many train trips to Toronto I could have afforded, or how many nights I could have spent in Vancouver at that cheap Delta Airbnb. I'm thinking about Blake and how we were flirting non-stop before I left, and whether I could have hooked him if I'd stayed in town. It's not his fault he forgot about me – after all, we weren't really *a thing* yet.

I don't know if I'm mad at my friends or myself. Truth be told, I would love to get away from them. I felt less claustrophobic in that dingy ship museum than I do on this beach. I fake a smile as Shanelle walks up to my patch of sand, still dripping saltwater. She'd probably rather be back there right now, but she feels duty-bound to check up on me. "Hey girly – still sick?" She sees the phone in my hand, and her expression changes to one of alarm. "That'll overheat out here," she says. She's not wrong. I may as well be holding a sauna rock.

"I just want to know that he knows," I reply nonsensically.

"That he knows what?"

"...that I know." I sigh, realizing how absurd I sound. "I'm not a moron," I add, defeated.

"Of course not."

"I just wish he hadn't strung me along. If he'd told me he wasn't interested, or wasn't ready..."

"He's a snake."

"Yeah," I agree, but I can't quite bring myself to believe that. Not yet, at least.

She scooches down to sit next to me, her face crinkling. The sand, not quite settled from yesterday's windstorm, is lumpy and uncomfortable. I sensed some buried litter underneath this patch when I first sat down, but was too preoccupied to find a nicer spot. "We've all been there," she says sympathetically. "I spent three years of undergrad hopelessly in love with one of my best guy friends, who totally didn't like me like that. I think that's why I did so well in school – I didn't have any actual dating to distract from my studies..."

But I've stopped listening, diverted by another unidentified object. "Do you see that?"

Something grey and bulbous is drifting through the air, balloon-shaped and solid, revealing no trace of the sky behind it. The atmosphere is windless, but the thing is moving at a decent clip along the beach, travelling in our direction.

Shanelle squints into the sun. "It's a cloud," she says.

She doesn't understand the implications, but that's for the best. There's a reason I directed her to the sky and not the ocean: the cloud obscures what's really floating up there. Its reflection in the water is clearer.

* * *

"It hurts to like, exist."

Brooke has the reddest, angriest sunburn I've ever seen, having foregone sunscreen in an ill-advised attempt to tan. She's been picking at her flaking skin since before we got to the restaurant; Shanelle swats her every time she does. I'm amused by the whole thing, which I know isn't fair or charitable – after all, it's not Brooke's fault that Blake's been a dog. But she could have been less flippant about it.

Jamie's been buried in her phone since we sat down. At first, she was frantically Googling pharmacies that may still be open after dinner; she's now given up on that and is searching for home remedies. "They say oatmeal works."

Shanelle scoffs at the idea. "Respectfully, if we can't find *lotion* – in a beach town! – where are we going to find oatmeal at 8 PM?"

"I think grocery stores are open late?"

"Maybe Brooke should suffer the consequences of her actions," I blurt out. I immediately feel three sets of eyes fix on me in horror. *Shit.*

"And what's that supposed to mean, Skylar?" Brooke asks, her voice like flint.

Shit shit shit.

I try to play it off as friendly ribbing. "That's what happens when you don't wear sunscreen," I say, but the teasing tone curdles on my tongue. "I mean, have you ever had a tan? Is it even possible?"

I'm a stand-up comedian bombing in front of a hostile crowd. Every word digs me deeper; I can feel the sand shovelled down my throat. Anger flares inside me. Brooke's pissed at me – whatever. As if she's the first person to ever have a sunburn. But why are Shanelle and Jamie looking at me like that? What do they have to be offended at? Why doesn't one of them chime in to tell Brooke to lighten up, make a joke to break the tension, *something*?

Or are they tired of taking care of me, now? Has my sulking and fear and panic finally exhausted their empathy? Sure, fair enough. But Brooke's fucking sunburn is worth coddling?

I came here for you, I want to scream. *I don't want to come here ever again.*

Instead, I take one last stab at reconciliation. If this one doesn't work, I'll run sobbing to the bathroom and email the travel agent and beg for an earlier flight. "Besides, I know a quick and easy method to kill the pain."

"And that is?"

Like a miracle, a waitress brushes by our table just in time for me to get her attention. "Can I buy a round of shots?"

* * *

My friends are easily bought. The mood around the table improves as soon as we down a round of a sickly sweet blue-hued concoction dubbed "the porn star."

"That was actually delicious," Brooke says, wiping her lips. "But the name's a little cringey."

"The names of alcoholic beverages are either sexual or violent," Jamie says, with the world-weary wisdom of a club-hopper with a Women's Studies degree. "Porn star. Blow job."

"Sex on the Beach. B-52," I add.

"Irish car bomb."

"Muff dive."

"That's a blow job shot."

"Is it?"

"Yep. Same thing."

"Isn't there a beer called Farmer's Daughter?"

"I thought that was a cocktail."

"I think it's both."

My eyes – and my thoughts – drift as I run out of names to contribute. This restaurant is the most transparent tourist trap on the strip, serving a mix of unbelievably fresh fish and oysters in addition to a deep-fried all-you-can-eat buffet. Really, though, we chose it because of the giant plaster crab perched over the door, ten feet long from end to end, its front claw extended in a gallant gesture of welcome. The interior is no less true-to theme: the live edge walls are bedecked with seashells and ship's wheels and multicoloured sand art in cheap wooden frames; barnacle-crusted boots and black-and-white photos of schooners; lobster traps and telescopes and massive taxidermy fish. Some of the fish sing.

I wonder if the staff get bored of it – if they roll their eyes at the throngs of tourists who somehow think this is an authentic place to eat. If the owner were here, he'd probably have to stay in character, like the Captain; use phrases like "catch of the day," as if the frozen fish sticks came directly off the boat. It must get exhausting to have to perform like that, playing a caricature of yourself seven days a way.

"I'm kind of disappointed we didn't see something like this," Jamie says in the distance. "Skylar, take a look." She shoves her phone in front of my face; I take it in my own hand, holding it steady while I watch the video on the screen.

It's a one-minute clip, something that's gone viral on Twitter. The sense of recognition is immediate: pristine ocean waters, the heavenly cerulean hue distracting from the powerful waves whisking human bodies twenty, thirty feet above sea level. Sunburnt tourists in bathing suits. This could be our beach. I lay my finger on the side buttons to turn the volume up, holding the phone as close to my face as possible. The video's been overlaid with a lush instrumental track, dreamy synths and vague chanting cut with noodling strings and tinkling bells. It's a generically ethereal jingle that would have come free with the video editing software, but it has a certain hypnotic appeal. It sounds like streaks of sun filtering through the waves and trickling towards the ocean floor, or the churning roar of the sea condensed into a souvenir bottle.

The video restarts and its focus becomes clear. Batlike shapes begin to form in the waves, sailing over the shoulders of the oblivious tourists. A school of manta rays, dark and rhombus shaped, their wingspans almost twice the length of that of the swimmers.

I feel a presence behind me. "O-M-G, how do they not notice?" Shanelle squeals. "Stop hoovering, Skylar, let me see!" I hand her the phone and excuse myself, rising from my chair and heading stiffly towards a sign that says, "Poop Deck."

"You okay?" Jamie calls. I nod without looking back.

The bathroom is shaped like an overturned lobster trap, the stalls draped with thick netting from fishing boats, which doesn't exactly make me feel less enclosed. Squatting over the toilet lid, I will myself to not imagine myself as one of those doomed tourists, far from shore and surrounded by stingrays. I tell myself that the rays are harmless, because the video wouldn't have gone viral that way if anyone had been seriously hurt. I try not to imagine what would happen if the rays did decide to attack, and what it would feel like to try to drag myself through the water, thick like sludge, as an angry aerodynamic thing glides towards me like a predator bird.

My phone buzzes; I almost drop it in the toilet as I withdraw it from my pocket. I can't think of any message that I could possibly care about in my current state, but I build it up anyway: if the message doesn't shatter the earth and crack the mirror, it will be a disappointment.

Surprisingly, it isn't.

My last text, sent six hours ago, had said, "Why did you lead me on?"

Blake's reply is almost a non-sequitur: "Everything I said was the truth."

Reading it snaps me from panic to anger. "When you said you were into me?" I shoot back, fingers flying so quickly across the keyboard that only autocorrect saves me from utter incoherence. "That was the truth?"

Blake's response is more bullshit: "I'm very interested in you."

"Liar," I hiss, wishing he could hear but not caring if anybody else does.

Masochistically, I open Instagram and search for his handle. The most recent photo is him with that bitch, mugging for the camera against a backdrop of willow trees, her make-up free with tousled hair hidden under a baseball cap, his red face streaked with sweat. I'm about to screenshot it and send it back to him triumphantly when I read the caption: "When you've been out of service for 48 hrs and your phone blows up." Posted less than a minute ago.

Calm down and think clearly, Skylar. Perhaps Blake *could* be sending me rapid-fire texts while simultaneously posting to the internet. Even if his phone is, as claimed, vibrating off the hook with a million other messages. But how could he have been "out of service" the last few days when–?"

My hands feel numb. Returning to texts, I type his name and erase it. Finally, I just write: "Who have I been talking to?"

The reply is almost instant: "You need to get your mind off this. You should go to the beach."

I wait for the inevitable request for swimsuit photos, but it never arrives.

* * *

I do go to the beach.

I wait until the girls are asleep and can't ask where I'm going, pushing aside the rows of suitcases zipped primly shut in preparation for tomorrow's plane ride. I hope they don't miss that flight on my account. I turn the deadbolt as gently as possible, so only the most unavoidable squeak of metal on metal can be heard, cringing as the mechanism clicks out of place. The door doesn't even whisper as I push it open and shut it behind me. I pad down the hall barefoot, leaving my room key behind.

I don't feel safe until I'm in the elevator several floors down, where I know Shanelle or Jamie or Brooke can't poke their heads out the door and see where I'm going. They'll know eventually, if they think to check my phone. I've written it all out in a text message to myself. I even did them the favour of removing the password protection from my phone before I left it charging on the nightstand.

The beach, when I reach it, has been raked free of people. It's late enough, of course, that most of the tourists will have already returned to semi-drugged slumber amid their four-hundred-dollar-a-night beds. If there were any stragglers, they must have been sucked in by the sand. For the duration of the walk, my eyes don't leave the ground. It isn't until the tide laps against my toes that I cast my gaze upwards.

I see it, lit by its own light.

The fish's face is a gaping horror, mouth overflowing with needle-sharp teeth, its jaw drooping like the edge of a rotted pumpkin. Its scales are a greyish white that flashes with purples and blues, like mother of pearl - like the flesh of a corpse. The stem that sprouts tumor-like from its forehead, thrown into garish relief by the glare, is a stalk of green-purple cartilage almost twice the length of the fish's body, curved at the end with the weight of a dangling orb that glows like the bulb at the top of a lighthouse tower.

I understand now that the thing I saw in the water wasn't *in* the water at all, but a reflection of this thing far above us. A creature of another dimension that can't always be seen with human eyes, but will sometimes let the ocean reveal its majesty. Not a sea monster, but an ancient being that swims the void of space.

The stem snaps as I watch, sending the orb plummeting. My heart stops – but it's an illusion. The fish is just re-orienting itself, lowering its searchlight as its explorations take it closer to the earth. Closer to this beach. I'm suddenly struck by what those videos from science class omitted: after all, what would a deep-sea fish need a light source for, if not to hunt?

* * *

I shiver as a breeze skims across the shore. It shouldn't be so cold, but my t-shirt is soaked in a salty sweat. The angler is now looming over me. Every muscle in my body tenses like I'm about to break into a run, but the only movement is in my legs, shaking uncontrollably but not taking me anywhere.

The fish opens its mouth.

And inside is paradise.

I'm staring into a secret ocean, as black and infinite as the void of space. The glancing light of the orb casts strange shadows along its floor, suggesting rocks that jut like distended molars, cavities giving way to sunken caves. Caves I have seen before. And further down its throat, the lightning bug glimmer that can only be flickering schools of fish. From that throat comes a song, like the roar you hear when you put a conch to your ear; like the muzak of the manta ray video; like sirens on the rocks. Soundwaves displace oxygen as the ground pulses, sand dancing at my feet. It's like those nightclubs where your bones rattle and your heartbeat feels tied to the rhythm of the bass, so much that you fear your heart will stop when the music does. The sea beyond is a single pane of glass, transparent and perfect, the reflections of the stars and the orb and the underside of the fish clear and exact.

It shouldn't be this still, I think, the first time my mind has kicked against the glories I am witnessing. I feel ungrateful – but it just looks so much like a cardiac monitor going flat.

Perhaps the sea can sense my faithlessness, because the glass shatters. The surface refracts and folds in on itself, the water scrambling down two flat plains. I shriek as the ocean collapses into a whirlpool, reaching my hand towards it as if I could plug the hole. But the vortex is relentless; it won't stop until it drains the sea. What water does escape floats like raindrops in reverse, caught in the angler's orbit. The music crescendos as the corrupted atmosphere swirls around me, picking up sand and shells. I strain to keep my eyes open – it would be a sin to shut them, now – and see palm trees ripped up from their roots and sucked into the fish's gaping maw.

As the angler fish prepares to swallow me, and perhaps

the whole beach, I feel remarkably little regret. Still, I bend to pick up one last handful of the dry, soft sand, crinkling my toes to feel the earth beneath them. I know I won't have this sensation again, not until the day the beast has consumed enough of the world to create a new one inside itself, and I emerge from the darkened sea and feel my degraded lungs flair to life upon a desolate new shore.

I hold onto the sand until the wind is too strong to resist, then open my hand and let the grains join the maelstrom. Closing my eyes, I feel my feet leave the ground, my body submerged in airborne water. I open my mouth to let more in. The wind tears at my hair and rips my clothes off. I'm naked as I cross the threshold of the angler's throat. The joy is ecstatic.

I haven't felt this way since before the lifeguard dragged me by the foot from the world within the fish. Every day since, I've been unmoored; even the dreams were nothing but a taunting torture, leaving me bereft and mourning for this place that was meant for me – where I will be accepted as I am.

Perhaps I should have expected to change. After all, nothing human could live for long in such an environment.

The first stage is blissful. The water massages my legs and calves, gathering up folds of skin and pulling them lower, lengthening my limbs and flattening them into fins. Warm water soothes the pain as the bones in my feet break. I barely feel the sting as something slashes across my throat, slicing two sets of gills into either side of my neck.

Then comes the stomach acid, dousing me in agony, and my body wails and writhes with waves of all-consuming orgasmic pain. My epidermis disintegrates into clouds of dust; *fruit flies*, I think, as I open my eyes to a flurry of flaking flesh. I entwine my fingers and try to save my eyes, but the current rips my hands away from my face and pulls them up above my head. My melting forearms touch and fuse together, my hands and wrists locked permanently.

A few seconds too late, I realize that whatever shape I take here will be my final form. I stupidly kick my legs, trying to swim towards less savage waters, but my left calf hits the back of my thigh and affixes to it. Startled, I jerk my knee forward, inadvertently soldering it to my stomach. I'm off-balance now, and my body tips to the left. Though I resent the idea of spending eternity as a scrunched-up rhombus, I pull my right leg into the same position.

I can swim, at least, though my shortened back fin limits how fast I can travel. My upraised arms help at first, but it only takes a few minutes (or hours – who can tell?) before they go completely numb. At last, my hands can do nothing but hang uselessly above my head, bobbing with the heartbeat rhythm of the current.

The darkness makes it hard to gauge how restricted my movements really are. Where are the other swimmers, the ones I saw before being sucked inside? Are they deeper in the angler's bowels, or were they just a trick of the light - the glare of the orb glinting against teeth? I try to call to them, expecting to choke on acid water as my jaws part. But I can breathe, like I have been all along, and the sound that comes rolling out my throat and across my tongue is beautiful. I smile, if such an expression is still possible for me. I'll be accepted into the choir.

I push forward with a kick of my knees, using my conjoined hands to guide me. Not that I can see – my eyes still haven't adjusted to the darkness. *If I still have eyes.*

Out of the gloom, a light approaches. It's about as big as one of my fists used to be, before they merged into a single stump. I expect to see another fish following, but the orb is unaccompanied. The light is mine. I shut my eyes and let myself float, feeling the water grow warmer as the source of energy comes nearer. The orb lands atop my knuckles and settles there, burning a socket into my flesh.

I am a creature of the deep. My body is misshapen, legs frozen into fins; my head forever bent under my outstretched arms, eyes trained on the seafloor. A long stalk extends above my head, from which a light dangles. I am warped but sleek: every vestigial part of me has melted away. My lipless mouth gapes, all teeth; my skin is rough and scaly. The last bits of flesh to dissolve are my eyelids. When they go, I look upon my new domain to find the darkness has dissipated.

Beneath my luminescence, the seafloor glimmers like mother-of-pearl.

acknowledgments

I'm deeply grateful to Tony Anuci for bringing this book to life. Tony's long been a champion of indie horror and it was a delight to work with him!

Adrian Medina did an amazing job with the cover, evoking both tropical pleasures and cosmic unease. I would say it's exactly what I had in mind, but I couldn't have come up with something this cool.

This story would not exist in its current form without the advice of Chris Campeau, Steve Smith, and Ben Cirne, who read a very rough early version of this and helped shape it into something coherent. I'm also indebted to Kristian McKesey for letting me bounce ideas off him for 11 years and counting.

I'm lucky to have worked with many fantastic editors and publishers over the years. Special thanks to Ira Rat from Filthy Loot, Dean M. Drinkel from Demain Publishing, and Red from Alien Buddha Press.

Cheers to Lorde for putting out a creepy/beachy album just in time for revisions.

The primordial version of *Beach Vibes* crawled out of the sea during a hurricane season family trip to Myrtle Beach. I'm eternally grateful for my wonderful parents, Colin and Erin, who made me into a bookworm and instilled my love for storytelling (and who gave me many stories to tell). And for my brother Alexander, who gives no-nonsense feedback while validating my bizarro-logic interpretations of the world.

Finally, thanks to everyone who picked up this book. Dip your toes in the water and enjoy.

about the author

MADISON MCSWEENEY WRITES HORROR, Weird, and bizarro fiction.

She's the author of *The Doom That Came to Mellonville* (Filthy Loot), *The Forest Dreams With Teeth* (Demain Publishing), and the poetry chapbook *Fringewood* (Alien Buddha Press). Her short fiction has appeared in anthologies like *American Gothic Short Stories, His Soul's Still Dancing: A Nicolas Cage Inspired Fiction Anthology*, and *Zombie Punks, Fuck Off.*

Madison's a devotee of cult films, heavy metal, and genre fiction. When she's not doing any of those things, she's probably exploring museums or going on aimless walks through her home city of Ottawa, Ontario.

Find her at:

Website: www.madisonmcsweeney.com

Twitter: @MMcSw13

Bluesky: mmcsw13.bsky.social